Baby Beaver Rescue

adapted by Susan Kim, based on the screenplay written by Susan Kim
illustrated by Alexandria Fogarty, Little Airplane Productions

SIMON SPOTLIGHT/NICKELODEON
New York   London   Toronto   Sydney

Based on the TV series *Wonder Pets!*™ as seen on Nickelodeon®

SIMON SPOTLIGHT
An imprint of Simon & Schuster Children's Publishing Division
1230 Avenue of the Americas, New York, New York 10020
© 2009 Viacom International Inc. All rights reserved. NICKELODEON, NICK JR., *Wonder Pets*, and all related titles, logos,
and characters are trademarks of Viacom International Inc.
All rights reserved, including the right of reproduction in whole or in part in any form.
SIMON SPOTLIGHT and colophon are registered trademarks of Simon & Schuster, Inc.
Manufactured in the United States of America
First Edition 10 9 8 7 6 5 4 3 2 1
ISBN: 978-1-4169-8499-3

It was a beautiful fall afternoon. Outside, the breeze was cool and the leaves were twirling to the ground. Inside the little schoolhouse, Linny, Tuck, and Ming-Ming were resting in their cages when suddenly the red tin-can phone began to ring!

Ring ring! Ring ring!

The Wonder Pets jumped up, put on their hats, and rushed to answer the phone. They began to sing:

The phone!
The phone is ringing!
The phone!
We'll be right there!
There's an animal in
trouble somewhere!

Soon Linny and Ming-Ming were standing by the phone. But where was Tuck?

Ming-Ming marched over to the sink. Tuck was at the bottom. "Are you coming or what?" she asked.

"I think I'm stuck," said Tuck. No matter how hard he tried, he couldn't climb out.

"Look!" said Linny. "Someone pulled the plug. All the water ran out!"

"Let's turn on the water, Linny!" said Ming-Ming.

"Good idea!" said Linny. "But first we need to plug the hole. That way the water won't run out again."

Once the plug was in place, Linny and Ming-Ming filled the sink with water and Tuck rose to the top.

"Thanks, Linny and Ming-Ming!" said Tuck. "Now let's answer the phone."

Linny picked up the phone and listened.

"Oh, no," she said. "It's a baby beaver. Her dam is broken and the water is pouring out!"

"What's a dam?" asked Ming-Ming.

"A dam is something that beavers build to keep themselves safe!" explained Linny. "But this little beaver's dam has a hole in it! It could wash away!"

"Then we'd better hurry," said Tuck. "Come on, Wonder Pets!"

Linny, Tuck, and Ming-Ming rushed to change into their superhero outfits!
They sang:

Linny, Tuck, and Ming-Ming, too!
We're the Wonder Pets, and we'll help you!

Then the Wonder Pets built their Flyboat so they could fly to the beaver's lake.

"We are coming to save you, Baby Beaver!" called Ming-Ming as the Flyboat soared through the sky.

The Wonder Pets sang:

Wonder Pets! Wonder Pets! We're on our way!
To help a baby beaver and save the day!
We're not too big and we're not too tough,
but when we work together,
we've got the right stuff!
Go, Wonder Pets! Yay!

The Wonder Pets flew over a big lake. Tuck saw the baby beaver waving to them. "There's the baby beaver and her dam!" he said.

Sure enough, the dam had a big hole in it. Water was pouring out.

"The hole is getting bigger," said Ming-Ming. "We'd better hurry!"

"I know," said Linny. "Let's plug the hole. That way, the water will stop pouring out."

Ming-Ming had an idea. "I will plug the hole with my mighty bottom!" She flew up and stuck her bottom in the hole.

But there was too much water coming through. It wasn't long before—*pop!* Ming-Ming came flying out.

Suddenly there was a big noise. *Crash!* More leaves and twigs fell out of the dam and into the lake. Now the hole was even bigger! More water was rushing out!

"This is serious!" said Ming-Ming.

"We need something else to plug the hole," Linny said. The baby beaver pointed at a tree stump.

"The tree stump, of course!" said Ming-Ming. "But it looks heavy. How are we going to lift it into the air?"

"Do you remember the plug in the sink?" asked Tuck. "It had a long chain attached to it. If we tie something around the trunk, maybe we can lift it up."

"Great idea, Tuck!" said Linny.

Using teamwork, the Wonder Pets got going. Ming-Ming flew in the air with a long vine. She dropped one end over a branch. Down on the ground, Tuck and Linny tied it around the tree stump.

As the Wonder Pets and Baby Beaver worked, they sang:

What's going to work? Teamwork!
What's going to work? Teamwork!

The Wonder Pets pulled the tree stump high up into the air! "Now let's plug the hole!" shouted Linny.

Ming-Ming pushed the stump toward the hole in the dam. Then Linny, Tuck, and the baby beaver let the stump drop into the hole.

The stump fit perfectly, and the water stopped pouring out!

"We did it!" cried Tuck.

The baby beaver's mom arrived and hugged her little girl. "Oh, thank you, Wonder Pets! You helped my baby and saved our dam!"

"Oh, it was nothing, really," said Tuck shyly.

"Yes, it was," said Ming-Ming. "You saved the day, Tuck."
"And you know what that calls for," said Linny. "Some celery!"

Go, Wonder Pets! Yay!